SOME SWAHILI WORDS

Bahati
luck

Dalila
gentle

Haraka
haste, hurry, bustle

Jelani
mighty

Karibu
welcome

Khalfani
destined to rule

Mosi
first-born

Nassor
victorious

Pembe
ivory

THE
LION KING

FOLLOW THE LEADER

by Page McBrier

Illustrations by Laureen Burger
David Pacheco
Denise Shimabukuro
Raymond Zibach

Grolier Books

ISBN: 0-7172-8352-6

CHAPTER

"S ire? Sorry to trouble you again, but—" Zazu the hornbill tiptoed toward Simba. The Lion King lay stretched out on a rock, enjoying the noonday sun.

Zazu tilted his long beak from side to side. "Your Sireship?"

Simba looked up wearily. All day long, the animals had been coming to him with questions that needed answers and problems that needed solutions. The leopards wanted permission to climb the old baobab tree. One of the baby chimps had accidentally swallowed a burr. A zebra had kicked and accidentally opened up a termite's nest. When would he get some peace?

"What is it now, Zazu?" Simba asked his steward. "Have we got more homeless termites? Sick chimps? Climbing leopards?"

Zazu fluttered his wings. "It's those Cape buffaloes again. They're hogging the water hole. The hippos are hopping mad."

Simba frowned. "I thought I told those buffaloes to move over."

"The buffaloes show no signs of shuffling, sire," said Zazu. "You know how buffaloes can be. Big, nasty creatures."

Simba stared out at the wide grassy plain. From where he sat, high on Pride Rock, his kingdom lay spread before him. He saw miles of grassland dotted with trees, bushes, and muddy ponds. The Zuberi River meandered across the plain like a silver ribbon. Beyond the grasslands lay more volcanic hills like the ones that formed Pride Rock.

Simba turned to Zazu. "It's always something lately, isn't it? Please tell the buffaloes that if they can't share, they'll have to move to the river."

Zazu gasped. "But, sire! There are crocodiles in the river!"

Simba smiled. "I know."

Zazu flew off to deliver Simba's message.

Simba closed his eyes again and rolled onto his back. The sun felt hot. Toasty. Perfect for a royal snooze.

"Dad! Hey, Dad!" Simba's son, Kopa, ran up. He leaped onto Simba's chest.

"Oomph." Simba opened his eyes. He saw Kopa peering into his face.

"Let's wrestle, Dad. Huh?" Kopa bounced up and down. "We haven't wrestled since maybe this morning."

"That long, huh?" said Simba. He gently batted Kopa's head with his paw.

"Grrr. Put 'em up," Kopa said. He backed up, lowered his head, and charged.

Simba grabbed Kopa's head with his

front paws and rolled him forward playfully. "Think you're tough, huh?" Simba said. "Grrr."

"Sire. Sorry to interrupt again."

Simba glanced up and saw Zazu standing with an old baboon, the wise teacher and healer Rafiki.

"Hello, Rafiki," said Simba. "What is it, Zazu?"

"It's that snooty giraffe, sire," said Zazu. "The one I call Nassor the Nasty. He's fighting with the elephants now." He sighed. "He's always fighting with someone. Last week, it was the gazelles. The week before, he took on the cheetahs." Zazu shook his head. "Why would anyone want to take on a cheetah? You can't trust a cheetah."

Simba pushed Kopa off his chest and sat up. "So what seems to be the trouble now?"

"Nassor says the elephants are destroying the acacia trees. They're eating the bark."

"That wouldn't surprise me," said Simba. "But don't we have plenty of acacia trees?"

Rafiki spoke up. "Not as many as you think," he said. He leaned on his walking stick. "When your father was king, we had many more."

Kopa perked up his ears. "Where'd they go, Rafiki?"

He patted Kopa on the head. "The elephants destroyed many of them," he said. "Others were lost to disease and neglect."

"Dad," said Kopa. "You've gotta talk to those elephants before they wreck the trees."

"Can't it wait?" Simba asked. "I haven't had a minute to myself all day."

"You know what they say," said Zazu. "A king's work is never finished."

"Is that what they say?" asked Simba.

Kopa scampered off. " 'Bye, Dad."

In the distance, Simba heard a high barking voice. "Hup, hup, keep it up.

Hup, hup, keep it up."

Pumbaa the warthog marched into view. Timon the meerkat stood on Pumbaa's back, giving orders.

Simba gazed thoughtfully at his old friends. When Simba's father, Mufasa, had been killed, Simba had run away because he'd thought his father's death had been his fault. Simba had been rescued by Timon and Pumbaa, and he'd lived with them as outcasts until Simba's friend Nala discovered them. It was only later that Simba had learned Mufasa had been killed by his evil brother, Scar, who now ruled the Pride Lands with the help of the hyenas.

Nala had persuaded Simba to return to the Pride Lands. Simba had battled Scar and won, becoming the new Lion King. Not long after, he and Nala had become the parents of Kopa.

Now Simba watched, amused, as Pumbaa marched in time to Timon's voice. As he marched, his long tail stood

straight up and waved like a flag.

"Oh, no!" muttered Zazu. "Here they come."

"Company, halt," called Timon. He hopped off Pumbaa's back and saluted.

"Long time no see, Your Majesty," he said. He bowed deeply. "Where've you been? I haven't seen you in any of the old spots lately, if you know what I mean."

"He's been busy with official matters," Zazu said. Rafiki nodded in agreement.

"Gee, is that so, Chief?" asked Pumbaa.

"I'm afraid it is," Simba said. "There's so much to do lately. So many decisions."

"Yeah, well, all work and no play is no fun. Right, Pumbaa?" said Timon.

Pumbaa snorted. "Right, Timon. Simba, you should come hang out with us. Eat a few bugs. Rest up a little. You know. Like the old days." He burped.

"Like now!" Timon said. "We're going to find a nice big rock away from the noise and the leopards and—"

"Take a snooze," said Pumbaa.

"Sounds heavenly," said Simba.

"So what do you say?" asked Pumbaa.

"I'd love to—" Simba began.

"But some other time," said Zazu.

"Huh?" said Simba.

"The king has duties to attend to," added Rafiki. "Sorry, fellas."

"Aw, shucks!" Pumbaa said.

Simba glanced at Zazu, then back at Timon and Pumbaa. "Some other time, okay?"

"Work, work, work," said Pumbaa.

"You're getting to be a regular drudge," said Timon.

"Duty before pleasure," said Rafiki.

"That's okay, Simba," said Timon. "*Hakuna matata.* No problem, right?" He waved good-bye.

Simba watched his friends disappear into the grasslands.

"About those elephants, sire," said Zazu. "What do you wish to do?"

CHAPTER

2

Simba snarled. "What's the difference whether the acacia trees are saved today or tomorrow? Aren't kings allowed a break once in a while?"

Rafiki smiled. "It is true you've been working very hard lately. A rest would do you some good."

"It certainly would," said Simba.

"But," continued Rafiki, "your responsibilities must come first. That is the way."

"The way of what?" asked Simba.

"The way of all things," said Rafiki. He laughed. "Each of us has a task. Your duty is to see that this kingdom runs smoothly."

"And our duty is to see that you run smoothly," added Zazu.

"I'd run a lot more smoothly if I had some time for myself." Simba stretched his front paws. "Very well. Where do I find those elephants?"

"Down in the acacia grove near the water hole," said Zazu. "Shall we come with you, sire?"

"Not necessary," said Simba. "Maybe I'll check on the buffaloes on my way back." He flicked his tail and started off.

"Not a happy camper," Zazu said.

Haraka, an ostrich, rushed up. "Fellas! Fellas!" he cried. "Where's the king? Where'd he go?"

"He had business with the elephants," Zazu said. "Why? What is it?"

"Bad news. Bad news," said Haraka. He flapped his wings.

"Tell us," said Rafiki. Haraka's long legs got him around. Often, he was first to hear news in the kingdom.

"It's uh . . . uh . . . oh, golly. I want to get this right." Haraka pointed to his head and squeezed his eyes shut. "It's about the baboons!"

Rafiki leaned forward. "Baboons! Where?"

Haraka opened his eyes. "Fast Falls," he said. "No, wait. Make that Grass Walls. The baboons in Grass Walls are in big trouble."

"Why?" Rafiki asked.

Haraka flapped his wings again. "I knew you'd ask that. Um, let me think. Was it hyenas? No. Um . . . locusts? No, that was hyenas and locusts. Or was it locusts and lizards?"

"Haraka, think!" said Rafiki. "This is important!"

Haraka pranced up and down. "All I can say for sure is that the baboons in Grass Walls are in deep trouble. Gotta go. Gotta go." He sped off.

CHAPTER

afiki's brow wrinkled. "I must leave
right away," he told Zazu.
"Why? Where are you going?"
"You heard Haraka. The baboons are
in trouble. I must help them."
Zazu eyed Rafiki. "So far away?
Forgive me, Rafiki, but didn't you say
your knee was bothering you?"
Rafiki hobbled off. He didn't seem to
be listening. "I must go now."
"Wait," said Zazu. "Shouldn't you at
least tell Simba?"
"I'll leave that to you, Zazu," Rafiki
called over his shoulder. He picked his
way down the steep side of Pride Rock.

The two gourds tied to his walking stick bounced up and down.

"Oh, boy," said Zazu. "Mayday. Gotta do something quick. Rafiki's going to get himself into trouble."

Zazu flew into the air. He spotted Nala resting in the shade of a boulder not far off.

He floated down beside her. "I'm glad I found you. We need to talk."

Nala had been resting after a busy morning of hunting. Her amber eyes filled with worry. "Hello, Zazu. Is something the matter?"

"Haraka just told us there's trouble with the baboons in Grass Walls. Rafiki took off."

Nala sat up. "By himself?"

Zazu nodded. "A one-man operation."

"Does Simba know?"

"Not yet. He's off resolving a dispute between Nassor and the elephants."

Nala stood up. "I'll find Simba."

"He said he was heading for the

acacia grove by the water—"

Kopa came dashing around the corner. He slid into Zazu and knocked him off his feet. "Pow. Gotcha!"

"Aawk!" Feathers flew up in every direction.

"Kopa!" Nala said. "You know better than that!"

"Sorry," said Kopa. "I slipped."

Zazu smoothed his ruffled feathers. "Luckily, my dignity is still intact."

Nala smiled at Zazu. "I'm terribly sorry. You know how cubs can be. They get carried away sometimes." She stopped. "I was just about to ask . . . would you mind keeping an eye on Kopa while I'm gone?"

"Me?"

"I won't be long."

"But . . ." Zazu watched Kopa grin at him. "Oh, very well."

"You be good, okay?" Nala said to Kopa. She licked his face.

"Mom!"

Nala left to find Simba.

"What do you want to play, Zazu?" asked Kopa.

"How about dead?" said Zazu. "We both lie down and don't say a word."

"I'd rather play good guys and bad guys," said Kopa. "I'll be the bad guy, and I'm chasing the good guy."

"No!" said Zazu.

"Here I come, good guy. Ready or not," Kopa said. He crouched low and growled.

"No! No!" said Zazu, backing up.

Kopa showed his teeth and charged.

"Oh, I hate baby-sitting," said Zazu. "Help!"

Nala made her way down the side of Pride Rock. At the bottom, she came to the grassy plain.

Nala trotted along quickly until she reached the acacia grove. Nassor was arguing with Pembe the elephant. Simba stood between them.

"And furthermore," Nassor was saying, "I have never liked you elephants. Why must you always bunch together?"

Nala hurried over. "Simba!" she called.

"What is it, Nala? What's happened?"

"Haraka told Rafiki there's trouble with the baboons in Grass Walls, and Rafiki's gone to help."

"Grass Walls?" said Nassor. "That's far."

Nala nodded. "Simba, do you think Rafiki needs your help?"

Simba shook his mane. "I'm sure Rafiki can handle the problem. Besides, I need some time off. I'm starting to run on empty."

"But, Simba," said Nala, "Grass Walls is a long way away. What if Rafiki runs into trouble? He shouldn't be out there alone."

Simba hesitated. Then he shook his mane and said firmly, "No, Nala, I'm not going to Grass Walls, and that's final."

CHAPTER

ala's eyes widened. "But, Simba! What if he needs you? Are you forgetting your duty?"

Simba sighed. "Not forgetting. Only avoiding." He gazed into the distance. "You're right, Nala." He turned back to her. "Tell Zazu to keep an eye on things while I'm gone."

Simba looked up at Pembe. "And please remember to leave some bark on the trees."

"When will you be back?" asked Nala.

"I don't know," said Simba. "Soon, I hope."

Simba ran in the direction of Grass

Walls. He knew that baboons could travel great distances easily, but Rafiki had that bad knee. He'd travel more slowly. Maybe Simba could overtake him.

Simba galloped along through the grass, then up and over the hills. Soon, he came to an area where he'd never been. The trees grew more crowded. Thick bushes covered the ground.

Simba moved more cautiously now. He sniffed the air for Rafiki's scent. A leopard stared down at him from a tree. A lizard darted past his paws.

Simba caught Rafiki's scent. "That way," he said, heading deeper into the bush.

Where was Rafiki? Simba pushed his way through the branches carefully.

Then the bush opened up. Simba stood on the edge of a grassy field. He lifted his nose and sniffed.

A flock of storks took off not far from where he stood. Then Simba heard the thunder of charging hooves.

"Help!" someone cried.

Simba scanned the field. "Rafiki!" he shouted.

A rhinoceros was chasing Rafiki. He had dropped his walking stick and was hobbling toward some high rocks.

The rhinoceros lowered his head and closed in. Rafiki stumbled and fell. He tried to get back up.

Simba roared and bounded through the grass. He cut off the rhinoceros as he was about to catch up to Rafiki. Rafiki

got up and limped toward the high rocks.

Confused, the rhinoceros stopped dead. Rhinoceroses have bad eyesight but excellent hearing. This one snorted and swiveled his ears, trying to find his target.

"Over here," Simba said. He stood off to one side, ready. His tail swished back and forth. "Here I am. Come and get me."

The rhinoceros wheeled about and charged.

Meanwhile, Rafiki had climbed up

onto the rocks, where the rhinoceros couldn't reach him.

"This way, Simba," shouted Rafiki.

Simba raced toward the rocks. The rhinoceros was madder than ever.

"Hurry," yelled Rafiki. "He's catching up!"

Tired from his long journey, Simba felt himself slowing down. Would he make it in time?

CHAPTER

The rhinoceros's hooves grew louder.

Simba focused on the rocks. Only a little farther. Using his last bit of strength, he lunged forward. Then, just as the rhinoceros reached him, he leaped onto the rocks.

"You made it!" Rafiki said. They scrambled higher for safety.

Below them, the rhinoceros came to a stop. When he didn't smell or hear anyone, he turned and lumbered off.

"Whew, that was close." Simba stared at Rafiki. "Are you all right?"

"Nothing broken," Rafiki said. "Good

thing you were here." He turned his head quizzically. "Why are you here, anyway?"

"I should be asking you that question," said Simba. "I heard the baboons in Grass Walls were in trouble."

Rafiki stared into the distance. "Grass Walls is my homeland," Rafiki said. "If the baboons are in trouble there, then I must go to help them."

"I never realized that Grass Walls was your home," said Simba. So much about Rafiki was mysterious. He spent a great deal of his time wandering and gathering herbs for healing.

Rafiki stood up and dusted himself off. "It isn't much farther." He had a faraway look in his eyes.

"I'm coming with you," Simba said.

"Are you sure?" said Rafiki. "I don't know what trouble awaits us."

"Rafiki," said Simba, "you have watched over my family ever since my grandfather, Ahadi, was the Lion King. Of course I'm coming with you."

"Very well," said Rafiki. He pointed to a distant set of hills. "Beyond those hills lies Grass Walls. It is a lush place full of wonder and beauty."

"It sounds magnificent," Simba said. "I can't wait to see it."

"Neither can I," said Rafiki. "I haven't been back for some time now. I don't know whether anyone will remember me."

Simba helped Rafiki retrieve his walking stick, and then the two of them set off. They traveled the rest of the afternoon. By the end of the day, they had reached the hills.

As they made their way up a wall of rocks, Rafiki said, "Once we reach the top of this plateau, Grass Walls will lie before us."

Rafiki reached the top first. He smiled as he looked out at his homeland. Then he rubbed his eyes. "Oh, no!"

"What is it?" asked Simba, scrambling up beside him.

Rafiki shook his head. "What has

happened to my home?"

Instead of a green valley, Simba saw a parched and dusty landscape. Instead of leafy trees, he saw bare ones that looked like skeletons.

Rafiki hurried down the face of the plateau. "Something is wrong," he said.

Simba followed him to the valley floor. The air smelled stale. Nothing stirred.

Rafiki leaned down and picked up a handful of red dust. He sifted it through his fingers and let it fall.

Rafiki and Simba walked along slowly, kicking up powdery clouds of dust. Every now and then, they came to a withered patch of grass.

"Where is the baboon troop?" Rafiki muttered. "What has happened to my family?"

"I don't see any signs of life," said Simba.

"We must go to the Great Pond," Rafiki said, "where everyone gathers."

The pads of Simba's paws were

burning. He was tired from their long journey. What had happened to Grass Walls?

They passed a clump of dry bushes. "Look there!" said Rafiki.

Far off, Simba could see a spot of shimmering water.

"It's them. There they are." Rafiki hobbled forward.

When they reached the Great Pond, Simba saw that it was the size of a big puddle. A few baboons huddled around the water. Others lay in the little shade under the bare trees.

"Rafiki!" a baboon called out. "Is it you?"

"Hello, Bahati," Rafiki called back.

Rafiki greeted several other baboons by name, then approached a baboon trying to wash her baby's hands. "Dalila! What has happened here?"

Dalila lifted her sad eyes. "We have no water, Rafiki," she said. "Everything has dried up."

CHAPTER 6

"Where is your leader?" said Rafiki. "You mean your cousin Jelani?" said a young baboon leaning against a tree. He laughed scornfully. "He'd just as soon let us die."

Rafiki stood up tall. "Take me to him," he said. "Take me to him now."

Dalila staggered to her feet. Her baby clung to her belly. "There, there," she said to the baby. "Hang on tight. We're going to find Jelani." She took off slowly on all fours with her baby swinging beneath her.

Simba and Rafiki walked beside her. They saw more baboons lying under leafless bushes or beside the path. They looked thin and tired.

"Tell me about Jelani," said Rafiki to Dalila. "How long has he been the leader?"

"A long time," she said. "Ever since Khalfani was killed by a leopard."

"Khalfani was a wise leader," Rafiki said.

"Indeed he was," said Dalila.

A shrill cry filled the air. "Rafiki! Is it really you?" An old baboon came limping forward.

Rafiki strained his eyes.

The baboon came up and grasped Rafiki's hands. Her coat looked dull and shaggy. Nevertheless, she gazed at Rafiki and gave him a toothless grin. "Don't you know me anymore, Rafiki?"

A smile spread across Rafiki's face. "Karibu!" he said. He turned to Simba. "This is my cousin Karibu. We played together when we were young. Karibu could hunt bird's eggs better than anyone in the troop. Karibu, this is Simba, the Lion King."

"Pleased to meet you," said Simba. "Tell us what has happened here."

"Our water supply has nearly dried up," Karibu said. "The other animals left long ago. There's nothing more to eat."

"But why hasn't Jelani found you a new dwelling place?" asked Rafiki.

"My nephew Jelani is a lazy leader, and he only cares about himself," Dalila cried.

Simba and Rafiki glanced around. How could anyone be that selfish?

"We're on our way to find Jelani," Rafiki told Karibu. "Have you seen him?"

Karibu pointed. "He's lying under that tree," she said.

Rafiki stalked toward the tree. Simba, Karibu, and Dalila followed behind.

A big baboon lay resting against the tree trunk. Several young baboons played in the dust beside him.

Rafiki stopped in front of the baboon. He looked young and strong. Simba and the others stood back to watch.

The baboon's eyes were closed. "Jelani?" asked Rafiki in a loud voice.

The baboon opened his eyes. "Yeah. What about it?"

"I am Rafiki, your third cousin once removed. Grass Walls is my homeland."

"Welcome home, cuz," said Jelani. He yawned and closed his eyes again.

"It's not a good welcome," said Rafiki. His voice trembled. "Since I was last here, much has changed. My people are no longer happy or well fed. The water is gone. The other animals have left."

Jelani shrugged. "Things happen," he said.

Rafiki pounded his walking stick on the ground. "Why haven't you taken the troop to another dwelling place?"

Jelani opened one eye. "'Cause I don't feel like it, okay?"

"Not okay," said Rafiki. He turned back to Karibu. "Why hasn't anyone challenged him?" he asked.

"They've tried," said Karibu. "He won't let anyone else take charge. He's still the strongest baboon in the troop."

"But . . ." Rafiki gazed around helplessly. He reached down and shook Jelani's shoulder.

Jelani opened his eyes with a start. "You again? Listen, I'm busy right now, okay? Leave me alone, Grandpa."

"Grandpa?" said Rafiki. He clenched his fists. "It's time you learned to be a proper leader."

Jelani stood up. He towered over Rafiki. "Oh, yeah?"

"Easy, Rafiki," called Simba.

With a shaky voice, Rafiki said, "I demand that you find your troop a new source of water."

Jelani leaned down. "Is that right? Who's gonna make me?"

Rafiki planted his feet firmly in the dust. "I am," he said.

CHAPTER 7

Rafiki turned to the crowd of baboons that had gathered around him.

"We will be leaving soon for a new dwelling place," he said. "It is time to go from this land."

"But the journey will be long," a young baboon cried out. "Many of us are sick. Who will lead us?"

"I will," said Rafiki.

The crowd buzzed.

Jelani's booming voice broke through the noise. "Not if I can help it," he said.

The crowd moved back. Rafiki stood alone, facing Jelani.

Rafiki rattled his walking stick in Jelani's face. "Stay where you are," he warned.

Jelani roared with laughter. "What are you going to do? Hit me with your cane?"

Simba broke through the crowd. "If it were up to me," he said, moving toward Jelani, "I'd just chew on your toes for a while."

Jelani stepped back. "Hey! Where did you come from?"

"I'm Simba, the Lion King of the Pride Lands. I understand you're moving your troop."

Jelani made a face. "It's a lot of work to move," he said. "Besides, it'll rain soon enough."

Simba roared. "Not soon enough for me," he said. "We're leaving first thing in the morning. Are you coming or not?"

Jelani swallowed. "I guess so," he said.

Simba and Rafiki smiled at each other. "I thought you'd see it our way," said Simba.

The crowd moved away. Rafiki patted Simba's back.

"Where shall we take them all?" whispered Simba.

Rafiki smiled mysteriously. "Don't worry so. I once found a place in my travels which I thought my troop would like. It's quiet and protected."

The baboons were up early the next morning. When Simba opened his eyes, he saw Rafiki under an acacia tree. Rafiki took a gourd off his walking stick and opened it up. He scooped out a handful of ointment and spread it on the palms of his hands and the bottoms of his feet.

Simba remembered that when his cub Kopa was born, Rafiki had spread that same kind of ointment on his forehead.

"Rafiki, what's that for?" asked Simba.

Rafiki looked up and smiled. "Today we will need a little extra help," he said.

The baboons were soon gathered and ready to leave. Young and old, male and female, they stood together, waiting.

Rafiki pulled them into a circle. Humming, he carefully dabbed the ointment on each baboon's hands and feet, even Jelani's.

When he finished, he said, "We must go now." He held his walking stick up to the sun. "That way," he said, pointing west. "Toward our new home."

The baboons started walking. Rafiki took the lead, and Simba took the rear. For most of the morning, the group moved at a good pace.

Soon, however, the sun became hotter.

"Mommy, I'm thirsty," cried a young baboon. "When will we be there?"

Rafiki gazed into the distance.

"Can't we take a rest?" said Dalila. "I'm weak from no food."

"We must keep going," said Rafiki. "We have far to travel today."

They continued across the dusty plain. The sun beat down. The air was still. The baboons moved more slowly now. A vulture in a tree stared down at them.

Even Simba felt exhausted. Karibu, at Simba's side, was puffing.

"What I wouldn't give for a cool, deep river and a shady forest right now," Karibu said. "I feel so unprotected out here."

Simba shifted his eyes from right to left. "Yes, I know."

They passed through a grove of leafless acacia trees.

Karibu glanced up. "Watch out!" she cried.

From high in the branches of the acacia, a leopard who had been lying in wait pounced. He landed on Dalila's back.

Shrieking and barking, the rest of the baboons scattered. Dalila's baby fell to the ground.

"Mommy!" he yelled.

The leopard picked up the baby baboon in his mouth and ran off.

"Mosi!" Dalila screamed.

"Mommy! Mommy!" shouted the little baboon.

That could be my own child, my Kopa, thought Simba. What if that were Kopa? Without another thought, he took off after the leopard.

Leopards can run very fast, but Simba resolved to run faster. He chased the leopard across the dusty plain.

They came to a dry riverbed. When the leopard paused to spring across it, Simba pounced. The leopard dropped Mosi, and the two big cats struggled. They rolled around in the dust, snarling and clawing. The leopard curled his lips and showed his sharp teeth.

Simba snarled. "Stay away," he said. With his powerful paw, he swatted the leopard across the ground.

The leopard rolled to a stop. He stared at Simba and hissed. Then he turned and slunk off.

Simba went up to Mosi. "Are you all right?"

Mosi nodded.

"Come on, then," said Simba. "Let's get you back to your mother. We still have a long trip ahead of us."

Simba picked Mosi up by the scruff of the neck and trotted back to where the troop waited anxiously.

"Mosi!" Dalila cried. The other baboons crowded around the mother and baby.

Rafiki approached Simba. "We must continue."

They trudged along slowly now. Even the stronger baboons, like Jelani, were dragging.

"Rafiki," said one of the mothers, "my baby is thirsty. We must have water."

"Soon," said Rafiki.

"How soon?" asked Karibu. "We can't go on. We're too weak."

"Soon," Rafiki said again.

Simba stared out at the dry plain. If they didn't find water soon, they would not be able to go on.

CHAPTER

8

Simba trudged along behind the last baboon. Where was Rafiki taking them?

He heard a cry, then someone shouted, "Rafiki! Come quickly!"

The baboons had stopped and were clustered around someone.

Simba hurried forward.

He saw Karibu on the ground. Her breathing was heavy, and her eyes were closed.

Rafiki knelt beside her. "Karibu! We must keep walking."

Karibu opened her eyes. "No, no. My walking days are over. Leave me

here. You must go on without me."

"I won't do that," Rafiki said. "Your time has not come yet."

Jelani pushed his way through the crowd. "Aunt Karibu! You must get up."

"No," she said. "I'm staying here."

Jelani reached down and gently lifted Karibu onto his back. "No, you're not."

The baboons grew quiet. Everyone stared at Jelani. "Well, come on," he said. "What's everyone waiting for?"

The pace picked up again. The landscape changed. There was grass here, but it was brown. The ground grew more hilly. The trees grew thicker. Then, in the distance, Simba saw cliffs.

Rafiki marched steadily on. The grass changed from brown to green. A flock of parrots flew overhead.

Rafiki stopped and held up his walking stick. He put his fingers to his lips. Then he tipped his head to one side and listened.

"What is it, Rafiki? What do you

hear?" asked one of the young baboons.

Rafiki's face broke into a smile. "Listen!"

"It's a waterfall!" said the young baboon.

"Water!" shouted another baboon. They all began talking at once.

"This way," said Rafiki, breaking into a fast hobble. "Right this way."

Rafiki led them into a thick forest canopy. Birds flew above. Monkeys chattered in the trees. Bugs sifted through the rich soil.

As they walked, the roar of water grew louder. A shaft of sunlight broke through the forest canopy. In the clearing, they saw the waterfall, a glorious torrent of water cascading down a cliff into a stream.

The baboons rushed forward. They waded into the water and drank in great gulps. The younger baboons splashed playfully. Jelani carried Karibu to the water's edge and gently lifted her down.

"How's that, Auntie?" he asked. "Feeling better?"

"Thank you, Jelani," she said.

Simba padded to the water and took a long, cool drink. He noticed Rafiki off to one side, watching. Simba went and sat beside him.

"We made it," Simba said.

Rafiki chuckled. "We certainly did."

That night, Rafiki and Simba rested by the waterfall with the other baboons. The next morning, Jelani came to them.

"I woke early," he said, "and explored the area. I've found a safe, protected spot just beyond the waterfall where the troop can live."

"You have changed," said Rafiki.

Jelani looked at the ground. "I was wrong to neglect my troop," he said. "I should have moved them long ago, but I was thinking only about myself, about how pleasant it was to lie around all day. Then yesterday, when I saw Aunt Karibu fall, I realized I had put us in great danger by not acting sooner. Everyone struggled to make it here, and they almost didn't. If it hadn't been for you and Simba . . ." He shook his head. "From now on, the troop comes first."

Rafiki nodded wisely. "I'm happy to hear that," he said. "Now you understand what it means to be a leader."

On the way back to the Pride Lands, Simba had time to think about what had happened. After they had walked for a long time, Simba said, "Rafiki, I've been thinking."

"Yes?" said Rafiki.

"Being the leader is an important job," Simba said. "It's not always easy."

"No, it's not," Rafiki said. "A leader has to take his responsibilities seriously."

"Especially a king," said Simba. "I was remembering how much I grumbled the other day about not having time off. But now I've seen what happens when a leader puts his own interests above those of his family and friends. Jelani had nearly let his troop starve to death."

Rafiki nodded. "But now he has learned that—"

"Your Majesty! Your Majesty!"

Timon and Pumbaa galloped into view. Timon was hanging on to Pumbaa's neck. They skidded to a stop in front of Simba and Rafiki.

Simba was alarmed. "What is it? Is everything all right?" he asked.

"Good thing you're back, Chief," said Pumbaa breathlessly.

"Why? What's happened?"

Timon wrung his hands. "We have a problem, and we need you to solve it," he said. "Like you did for Nassor the Nasty."

"What is it, friends?" asked Simba.

Timon spoke up. "Which do you think is better for a sore throat? Mashed beetle or ground chicory leaves?" Simba's jaw dropped, but Timon didn't notice. "I say chicory leaves—"

"No, no, no," interrupted Pumbaa.

"Nothin' like a couple of mashed beetles to get a sore throat back into shape."

Timon hooted. "Pumbaa! How can you say that?"

Simba growled to get their attention. "Quiet, you two!" He looked from one to the other. "Do you mean to tell me this is your problem?"

"It's a doozy, huh?" Pumbaa said.

Simba tried not to smile. "Now, let me ask you a question. Is anyone in danger?" They shook their heads. "Good. Are the Pride Lands in any trouble?" They shook their heads again. "Then, I think this is something you can work out by yourselves," he said gently. "All right?"

"You mean you can't help us?" Timon asked.

Rafiki interrupted. "The king is usually called in for . . . um, larger disputes."

"Oh, I get it," Pumbaa said. "On a scale of one to ten, this problem would be a minus fifty."

"Exactly," Simba said. "Sorry, fellas.

It's not that I don't care, but it's been a long two days. I'm on my way back to Pride Rock now, and if there are no serious matters waiting there . . ." He took a deep breath.

"Yeah?" said Pumbaa.

Simba smiled. "Then I shall find a nice warm rock and stretch myself out for a snooze."

"A well-deserved snooze, I might add," said Rafiki. "Once the basket is full, the hunter can eat."

Simba laughed, then turned to Pumbaa and Timon. "Care to join me?"

"Sure!" said Timon. He turned to Pumbaa. "I've been thinking. How about we call it even? When you get a sore throat, you can eat all the mashed beetles you want. When I get a sore throat, it's ground chicory leaves all the way."

Pumbaa grinned. "I can do that," he said. "*Hakuna matata*, right? No problem." He yawned. "You know, a snooze sounds good to me too."

They stared at Rafiki and Simba, who were walking ahead.

"Hey! Wait for us!" yelled Timon. "It's almost nap time!"

"And we don't want to be late," said Pumbaa. They broke into a run and raced for Pride Rock, passing Simba and Rafiki on the way.

"It's good to be home," said Simba.

"And very good to have a home to come back to," Rafiki said. "Hurry, Nala and Kopa are waiting for you."

"Will you excuse me if I run ahead?" Simba asked.

"*Hakuna matata*," said Rafiki.

Simba broke into a gallop and was soon out of sight.

Rafiki began to walk faster. "I hope I'm not too late for that nap."